E   Phillips, Sally
PHI
       Cake cake cake pie

DEMCO

Dear Parent:

Congratulations! Your child is taking the first steps on an exciting journey. The destination? Independent reading!

STEP INTO READING® will help your child get there. The program offers books at five levels that accompany children from their first attempts at reading to reading success. Each step includes fun stories, fiction and nonfiction, and colorful art. There are also Step into Reading Sticker Books, Step into Reading Math Readers, Step into Reading Write-In Readers, Step into Reading Phonics Readers, and Step into Reading Phonics First Steps! Boxed Sets—a complete literacy program with something to interest every child.

Learning to Read, Step by Step!

Ready to Read   Preschool–Kindergarten
• **big type and easy words** • **rhyme and rhythm** • **picture clues**
For children who know the alphabet and are eager to begin reading.

Reading with Help   Preschool–Grade 1
• **basic vocabulary** • **short sentences** • **simple stories**
For children who recognize familiar words and sound out new words with help.

Reading on Your Own   Grades 1–3
• **engaging characters** • **easy-to-follow plots** • **popular topics**
For children who are ready to read on their own.

Reading Paragraphs   Grades 2–3
• **challenging vocabulary** • **short paragraphs** • **exciting stories**
For newly independent readers who read simple sentences with confidence.

Ready for Chapters   Grades 2–4
• **chapters** • **longer paragraphs** • **full-color art**
For children who want to take the plunge into chapter books but still like colorful pictures.

STEP INTO READING® is designed to give every child a successful reading experience. The grade levels are only guides. Children can progress through the steps at their own speed, developing confidence in their reading, no matter what their grade.

Remember, a lifetime love of reading starts with a single step!

For Hunter, with love

www.stepintoreading.com

Educators and librarians, for a variety of teaching tools, visit us at
www.randomhouse.com/teachers

Library of Congress Cataloging-in-Publication Data
Phillips, Sally Kahler.
Cake cake cake pie / by Sally Kahler Phillips.
    p.   cm. — (Step into reading. Step 1 book)
SUMMARY: Simple rhyming text and illustrations depict a silly series of events that keeps a young
boy from eating his cake.
ISBN 0-375-82929-6 (trade) — ISBN 0-375-92929-0 (lib. bdg.)
[1. Cats—Fiction. 2. Dogs—Fiction. 3. Stories in rhyme.]
I. Title. II. Series.
PZ8.3.P558215Cak   2004   [E]—dc22   2003018368

Printed in the United States of America   First Edition   10 9 8 7 6 5 4 3 2 1

STEP INTO READING, RANDOM HOUSE, and the Random House colophon are registered trademarks
of Random House, Inc.

Cake Cake Cake Pie

By Sally Kahler Phillips

Random House New York

Cake.

Cake.

Cake.

Pie.

Cakes.

Cat.

Oh, my!

Partly dressed.

Partly bare.

Shirt.

Pants.

Underwear.

Scarf.

Coat.

Shoes.

Hat.

Dog.

Dog.

Dog.

Cat.

Very high.

Very tall.

Thin.

Big.

Fluffy.

Small.

People.

Pet.

Pet.

Pet.

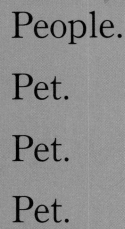

Fireman.

Fire truck.

Thank you!

Vet.

Cozy house.

Cozy street.

Home again.

Time to eat.

Hair.

Ear.

Neck.

Head.

Pillow.

Sheet.

Blanket.

Bed.

All asleep.

All awake.

Yum! Yum!
Breakfast.
Cake!